I0712767

The Elephant's Trunk that Kept Growing

Written by Lesley Ostapa

One day I went to the zoo with my family.
I was very excited to see all the different animals.
The first enclosure we got to were the elephants!
I pulled my parents over.

Zoo

As I was watching them,
one of the elephants
looked directly at me.

My hands began to tingle.

Oh no, is it going to happen again?

I quickly looked at my parents.
They were busy talking to the zookeeper.
When I turned back, the elephant still had its eyes on me,
but something strange was happening – its trunk
was growing longer, and longer,
and longer!

"Mom, can you see?" I asked.

"Just a minute, I'm talking."
She didn't turn around.

"Hop on!" the elephant said.
And, before I knew it,
the elephant swept me up on his trunk

and we set off out of the enclosure!
I was so high I could see all the amazing animals.

We came to the panda area.
The elephant carefully set me down inside it.
I ran up to the top of a cave and watched the fluffy animals
closely while they played and ate.

One of the pandas climbed a tree
and gazed down at me.
It was out of this world.
I had never seen anything like it!

Next, the elephant took me to see the monkeys.
They played together mischievously.
I enjoyed watching them swinging from tree to tree.
Oh, how I wished I could swing with them.
They looked like they were having so much fun!

Next, I hopped on the elephant's trunk
and visited the giraffes.
Instead of lowering me to the ground,
the elephant set me down on...
the neck of one of the giraffes!

We ran through the grass.
It stopped by an apricot tree to eat some leaves.
I bit into a juicy apricot!

I felt so lucky to be visiting
all these different animal enclosures,
encountering all the magnificent animals.
I normally wouldn't get
to interact with them like this.

"Let's have even more fun before I take you back!"
the elephant said.

He put me down by a pool with sealions.
We jumped in. The elephant
splashed me with his trunk,
squirting water everywhere.

The sealions swam all around me, making lots of loud noises.
They were very friendly.

I had so much fun, but it was time to go
before my family started worrying.
I wondered what they would say when they saw us!

When we got back to the elephant enclosure,
my family was STILL talking to the zookeeper!

The elephant lowered me to the ground.

"Mom!" I tugged on her sleeve.

"My goodness! Why is your hair wet?"

"The elephant with the big trunk
picked me up and we went for a swim
with the sealions."

"You sure have a wild imagination,"
Mom said, looking at the elephant —
its trunk was the same size
as all the other elephants' trunks!

I felt my wet hair and smiled.

It was the best trip to the zoo!

The End

Words you might not know

Animal enclosure
- space that is closedvv for keeping animals inside.

Zookeeper
- a person who takes care of animals.

Gazed
- to look at something or someone for a long time.

Magnificent
- something that is incredibly beautiful or impressive.

Tingle
- a slight prickling or stinging sensation.

www.ingramcontent.com/pod-product-compliance
Lightning Source LLC
Chambersburg PA
CBHW041420300726

48981CB00007B/352